Contents

FORETOKENS

ALSO BY SARAH HOWE

Loop of Jade

FORETOKENS

Sarah Howe

Chatto & Windus
LONDON

1 3 5 7 9 10 8 6 4 2

Chatto & Windus, an imprint of Vintage, is part of the Penguin
Random House group of companies

Vintage, Penguin Random House UK, One Embassy Gardens,
8 Viaduct Gardens, London SW11 7BW

penguin.co.uk/vintage
global.penguinrandomhouse.com

Penguin
Random House
UK

First published by Chatto & Windus in 2025

Permissions acknowledgements are listed on p. 84.

Typeset in 11/14pt Minion Pro by by Six Red Marbles UK, Thetford, Norfolk
Printed and bound in Great Britain by Clays Ltd, Elcograf S.p.A.

The authorised representative in the EEA is Penguin Random House Ireland,
Morrison Chambers, 32 Nassau Street, Dublin D02 YH68

A CIP catalogue record for this book is available from the British Library

ISBN 9781784746131

for Saul and Willow

The dead don't die in us, but are laid down in successive strata of emptiness

– KARIN KARAKAŞLI

Calendar

Unearthed in a clear-out, a picture calendar she's kept
– hoarding, I've learnt, is a mark of the emigrant –

across continents and time. *Beautiful Hong Kong 1983*
reads the cover's winking skyline, not quite idiomatically.

The comb-bound pages, flipsides mottled, stick –
each month a panoramic vista shot from up the Peak

or other island spots, full-colour photography
faded now, tacky, as silk wallpaper Chinoiserie.

How quaint it seems, my birth-year, or how colonial:
Birthday of Her Majesty sits days from *Tuen Ng Festival.*

In January's foreground, an orange-tiled pagoda
pops from scrubby mountainside above the skyscrapers,

their bar-chart ranks washed-out against the harbour's blue,
where a haze of rain turns down the contrast on Kowloon.

A sense that something's off, then suddenly it dawns –
the tallest of the needles pinned through the coast are gone

or rather not-yet-there; the time-travel uncanny
like spotting the twin towers intact in an '80s movie.

I picture it: the waterfront a juddering time-lapse
where buildings fall and rise like the Hang Seng index

cocooned in a greenish shroud of scaffolded bamboo
to emerge at cloud-level, gleaming and improbable –

the sky's bright hemline creeping ever higher
while junks skim like fiery leaves across a pond's mirror.

Count back nine fingers: February. The month I sparked
into being, a whorl of cells. Another cliché: fireworks

like red anemones cast their glow over starlit water,
office blocks ghostly from the long exposure.

March: the green Peak tram chugs up a jungled incline.
I have eyelids now (still fused), a crescent moon of spine.

I flip ahead to June, which frames the exact aspect
from the windows of our family's long-gone flat:

once you've left, now turns into something foreign.
My kicks are butterflies, my length a handspan.

August: dusk, and the city's purpled high-rises
disappear beneath a glaze of sky in *famille rose*

to reinvent themselves in blinking neon,
as traffic streaks in white-hot ribbons.

By the last trimester, each puffing step's a strain;
life in slow-mo, freeze-framed to the finish line.

On October's spread, an orphaned clocktower
in reddish brick, marooned on a demolished shore.

Note how the 14th has been highlighted in yellow:
she did mention I was two weeks overdue.

December: a tyre-skirted ferry edges towards dock
caught in its endless crossing, back and forth, forth and back.

Waking

after W. S. Graham

These heavying months, my nights have bobbed in your wake –
quiet passenger in your heart-lulled craft, asleep
to the glaring world of after. Soon we will make

our introductions: this is called *home*, this a *tree*,
that bite at your cheek is *winter*. You can't yet hear
our voices' muffled cello; your dial's tuned to sea.

My steps lengthen and slow, but my fears lope before
me: laid out on a gurney, gut a sinking stone,
straining to hear the pitch of ocean at your door

to find the room silent: unthink it. I will take
each day by restless day until we hear your cry
rise among the liquid stars assembled as you wake.

Expect no logic from a pregnant woman

even one trained
in the arts
of argument &
as for arguments
there are lots
of those I can tell
you that for free.
Take that time I
screeched red-cheeked
in the volvo as he
steered us & the keen-
ing car seat towards
our shared destiny.
Picture this scene:
on the nightstand
sits a well-thumbed
copy of *How Not To
Hate Your Husband
After Kids*; a female
form grotesque dis-
tended lies beached
among heavy sheets
in the half-lit mind
of 5.25 a.m. & the wail
goes up *mummy
mummy mummy*
from the cooling
cotbed in the box
room as the radiator
starts to tick and fuss.

Is this the moment
for Mummy the philo-
sopher to doubt
the consciousness
of others assured
in the separateness
of our closed-off
bodies? Just as the
loaded breasts begin
to seep. I must stop
finishing his left-
over pasta soused
as it is in toddler
germs. Reason
dictates. At eight
months my body
is not my own.
My ration of sleep
will soon be eaten
almost away like my
vermiculate former
brain. Still the night's
deepest reaches do
give up their intu-
itions their *seeing-
ins* like flares at
the edge of pressed-
on eyelids. I have
made something
from this life just
don't ask me what

Songs Spun of Us

. . . A lphabet of us, cipher deciding the exact momen T

   G enes flip on. Pierced, an ovum's moon divides in syn C

      G aining distinctness, a spine's pale curl, the body's fabri C

   G rows symmetrical. At first the code will seem chaoti C:

G leaning sense means tuning our ears to another musi C

   A rchived deep in our being, filtering out the ancient rus T

      A nd scrap abandoned across its expanse. Imagine the firs T

   C ell nudging its notes to form carbon's accidental son G –

A lchemical soup in some blackened, deep-sea ven T

   A ngling towards life; a ladder of atoms beginning to twis T . . .

Undersong I

o w	om n
on vv	om s
ovum s	m oon
o mums	v mo on
o mom	mo v sun
o mums	mov on
mums o	mor son
mum so	mor on
ov ums	mor n
o mums	mo urn
o u	no urn

Sometimes I think

of the conkers I gathered once
                    when small myself
shucked of their green armour
                    and placed in
the glass bowl with the silvered
                    rim to admire
their mahogany sheen. Why am I
                    driving the train
off the rails? Two nights ago
                    my son woke
at four in the morning, crying
                    for me in the dark.
I placed my cool hand on his
                    forehead, licked
with winter clamminess. He said,
                    I had a bad
dream, softly, eyes tight shut, like
                    something heard
in a story. To my knowledge
                    his first – a concept
I'd thought he hadn't yet met
                    in his slender frame
of human experience. The CD
                    spinning leisurely
in the neighbour's ruined magnolia
                    glints its
ambit of tapering sun. As I kissed
                    his hair I had
a vision of his little head as a nut
                    or hollow shell.

A day or so later the conkers
                              issued a plague
of white wriggling worms from their seemingly
                              impermeable
glossy surfaces. Next morning over rice pops
                              I asked him
what he had dreamed. I listened like
                    ·   a mother
in a story, like listening could make it
                              right.

A History of My Relationship with My Mother in Twenty-three Arguments about the Laundry

In my parents' house the second-smallest room and my mother's every sixth waking thought is devoted to the laundry

Growing up a pair of my jeans frayed at the heel, a favourite jumper, would disappear for months it seemed, having been sucked into the faintly musty mountains of colour-coded, fabric-sorted, care-instruction-heeded, but as yet undone laundry

I started to wonder why, as a not exactly lazy teenager, I had never helped with the laundry

I started to wonder why there was always so much laundry

Until in my thirty-fourth year I moved back into my parents' house, though not my childhood room, bringing one husband one newborn and an awful lot of laundry

I didn't understand then how laundry didn't mean in any normal sense just laundry

I started to find neat piles of folded pastel sleepsuits pressed to perfection, or strung up in the airing cupboard on tiny hangers saved, it seemed, since my own babyhood, boxed and shipped halfway across the world, and something tugged in my stomach that wasn't about laundry

In time, it became, *Mummy, please don't do our laundry*

I would find her a staring, agitated zombie coming down for breakfast at nearly lunch and she told me that she couldn't sleep at night because she was waiting for the tumble drier to finish its cycle at some point past three, and if she did not wait for its *beep beep beep* there's always a chance it would burst into hidden arcing flames smouldering from the compressed greyish fluff spun from all our mortal hair and laundry

It transpired that she has an unshakeable belief in the need to load the drum no more than a quarter of the way, despite my protestations about killing the planet with laundry

Pushing the pram through the twilit park to let off steam my husband would growl, *She's crazy, it's not just the laundry*

I sought to illustrate to her that putting more than one towel in at once would not result in disaster, flood, famine or destruction of said laundry

As I said it, I recalled how friends at school had laughed at my pronunciation of that word, *ta-well*, with two syllables, picked up from a non-native speaker mother whose fingerpads were etched with brown cracks like drought-struck fields because of the sheer graft (*I'm not a wife, I'm a slave*) she devoted to household work like the laundry

Eventually the corner-heaps of socks and sheets and god knows what got too much and I spent a weekend with an eight-week-old in the forget-me-not sling at my chest, bending and lifting, bending and lifting, my heavied leaky body to cycle through load after load of fucking laundry

I worked my way down through ancient strata of crumpled clothing, socks stiffened as if in Everest permafrost, trouser legs splayed like victims at Pompeii, recognising revenants, fashion hauntings, till I reached towards the bottom a school cricket cap spattered with black spots and blotches my brother must have last worn shortly before puberty, which he'd tipped into the wicker basket and lost to the psychic trauma archaeology of laundry

In the eighth or ninth month we went away for a week, desperate for space, and my mother shrank to teddy size a woollen shrug of mine slung from the back of the guest-room door, putting it through a hot spin-cycle because *You said your clothes didn't need any special care, so I thought I'd help put it in the laundry*

In more time, it became if she would stay out of ours, I would stay out of her laundry

I am still amazed by the soul's opacity towards itself, as illustrated by our adventures in passive aggressive laundry

Stood in front of the ancient Miele dryer one night, she told me that as a child of five or six, when her mother couldn't afford to look after her and she was farmed out to live with other families, the way she earned her keep was to be in charge (she gestured to a welt I'd never noticed on her wrist) of their ironing, her small fist steering one of those old bronzed hollow ones loaded up with orange coals (a detail so absurd it almost made me laugh), and all the other family's assorted laundry

Sometimes, glancing up from his paper at the hangers perched on every knob, their untenanted shirts, my dad used to say, *This house looks like a Chinese laundry*

If there is a god who flits about and pities such shopworn tumbled souls as ours let it be the god of laundry

Now that I, husband, child one and now two, have our own home again, and she has hers, I think of her at night still sitting at the morning room table alone at three-thirty, in the reading lamp's illuminated pool, flipping through the *Radio Times* with a bevelled pink highlighter waiting for the *beep beep beep* too high-pitched for her ageing ears to hear that signals an end to the latest round of laundry

In the Chinese Ceramics Gallery

Earthenware Model of a Horse, Unglazed

I, too, am a survivor.
My eroded coat dappled with lichen and stars.
My spirited tail has long
snapped off.

One millennium and then another
has wheeled on by
since the potter squatting on his dusty stool
thumbed my jowls

to the perfect roundness – a gesture
tender despite his production line – and nicked
my nostrils in this haughty flare. 'Stocky'
they called me

in the catalogue. I admit,
though hollow, my belly's a swollen gourd, buddha-full.
Ears pricked, mane brush-stiff,
my grin is quizzical, sometimes

even a grimace
behind the smudgy glass.
My hooves were long
buffed by clay ranks of imperial grooms.

Reserved for only the finest tombs
my kind maps out the trade
between civilisations –
one squat stallion for fifty bales of silk.

They rolled out the Silk Road before us
all the way to the walled city of Chang'an. The Han
emperor sent for us to fill
his echoing stables. He called us his *Tian ma*,

'celestial horses', expecting our hardy stock
when the time came
at last to carry him up the narrow passes
into Heaven. Some nights

I dream
of galloping across scrubby plains, the herd's sweat
tart as highland apricots around me –
far blue peaks retreating into memory.

Porcelain Tea Caddy Painted in Underglaze Blue

Far blue peaks retreating into memory
as wizened cedars twist against a glaze

of sky . . . these whimsical scenes so finely
brushed across my surface resemble

nothing I've seen on my crossings. I watch
this latest well-heeled young gent press his suit

as they practise their pouring, the lily-
fingered daughters of the prosperous

Liverpool merchant who spotted me buried
on a stall of fans and girdles. A seafarer

come good, still he has an eye: a man
of taste, my owner. His girls will have all

the graces, proficient in the rituals
around this steaming, still-exotic brew

that measures out an empire's domain
while glancing, spout poised, from the corner

of an eye. I observe from my silver tray.
Where do you think it comes from, capital

to fill a townhouse like this? It's not just wares
like me trussed as cargo. Human beings are,

were always, things. You don't want to see?
He knows, my man of taste. Ask the sugar

bowl here what it is it sweetens. One day
the English will forget who invented tea.

Finely Potted White Glazed Porcelain Cup, Dehua Ware

The English will forget who invented tea.
The way you might not guess, at first,
who made me, or why. The riddle of my origins

begins on a spinning wheel in Fujian, and ends
across two continents, with a silversmith
in Restoration London. I was made once

in a kiln's stark flame, feeling the translucent
glaze harden at my lip. Once cool, I was ready
for the kiss of alcohol. On summer evenings

between friends I brimmed with rice wine
no less refined than my own pure moon –
this white the Chinese call *Dehua*, but you

might know as blanc de Chine. Some twists
in my provenance are lost even to me:
a Pope's embassy, the halls of Versailles,

hands that held me up to the light in awe
at my lustre; placed me in locked cabinets
with seahorses, sextants, unicorns' tails.

But somewhere along the way that clod
of a smith insisted on gilding the lily.
I still remember the grip of those red-hot

scallops clamped around my rim, the strange
weight of this metal foot: never again
will I rise for a toast, bright against the night's

black silk. Remade in your imagination:
a sugar bowl. The brittle lumps clink
against my delicately tapering sides

like coal into a pail. A creature of two
worlds, but belonging to none. Tell me,
is there a word for it in this new tongue?

Thinly Potted Porcelain Kraak Dish Painted in Underglaze Blue

Is there a word   for it in this new tongue?
The class of ships the Portuguese   named *caravela*,
and the French *caraque.*   Swift three or four-masters,
they were *kraak*   to the Dutch, whose guttural pitch
I first heard from the sailors   who loaded us up
in our straw-stuffed crates: *Porcelain   vessels of diverse sorts*
the manifest called us   stowed by the hundreds
of thousands. Wares   named for those stately ocean-
going craft   sailing homeward from the mythic East
freighted with silk and damask   barrels of oakum
quicksilver, cinnabar, camphor.   Till disaster struck:
wrecked   off Goa's golden coast. As the cold current
of decades flowed past us, my stacked brethren   crusted
with barnacles   and powdery salt, mouths filling up with
silt. Still, some of us continued to gleam   like the shells
that yawned in those depths.   Dredged up from the dark
they pieced my fragments   back to wholeness, masked
each crack   with filler and skill. At last I came to rest
in this museum: a heavy Victorian vitrine, whose subtly
distorting glass recalled for me light   filtering through
underwater weeds. That night   in the Blitz was my last
near escape. Nothing like the kiln's   clarifying flames
that fire was   something else: ranks of precious artefacts
blasted into tinder, their cases   smashed; rare specimens
reduced to scattered feathers, shards   of wired bone.
In the aquarium, fish boiled   in their tanks or swilled
down drains; the model fishing boats   went up in smoke.
I've seen what it takes   to cradle a wreck back to the light.
Leaving the fractures for all to see   they rebuilt this place.
From the other side of ruin   we found safe passage.

Pair of Incense Burners: Dogs of Fo

From the other side of ruin
A queer old pair, like two
you can tell by the ribboned
our left front paws. Widowers.
our *yang*, once dandled upturned
to signal their maternal sides.
a singed mane, a broken
you'd never guess from these
Panting, we proffer the leashes
as if bounding up for walkies.
ferocious guardians flanked
door or shrine, driving off
growl – or a puff of smoke
Thrust together by chance
muddle along. Two centuries
Not exactly native here
haunting your country piles
Most recently we took up
mantlepiece to sentinel
We did this duty solemnly
like secret service agents
As for that spell in the
there. We still shiver at
We are lions, you know.
misconception amongst
we do resemble pug-nosed
because our maker never
as he did on China's east
would stroke our backs
more flamboyant than hers

we found safe passage.
left shoes. Male and male:
balls we crook beneath
Our long-lost mates, *yin* to
cubs like eerie miniatures
Still, we're not unscathed:
spout, betray a tragic history
benignly dentured grins.
gripped between our teeth
You might forget our role:
either side of a traditional
ill-spirits with a deep-bellied
from the other end's hole.
or a canny auctioneer, we
on, we hardly ever quarrel.
we're adopted denizens –
while failing to blend in.
station on a dusty English
it seemed, a carriage clock.
heads erect, ready to leap
from our blocky pedestals.
museum store, let's not go
the sight of bubble-wrap.
The dog thing's a common
foreign ghosts like you. True,
shih-tzus, but that's simply
saw a lion up close, living
coast. The lady of the house
with their armoured plaits
admiring this fine green glaze.

Stoneware Dish, Longquan Kilns

Admiring this fine green glaze
      might bring to mind
      a lichened
mountain pine, undertones
      of grey and jade
ringed like tiny moons

      along its darker side.
Or the travellers among you
      might think
of the desert aloe –
      its pale spines
picked out by starlight

      and by camels
      bound
in caravans, scenting hidden
      veins of green
across the empty sand.
      Once upon a time

dishes of my shade
      were known as *celadon* –
      named for
a shepherd in a French romance
      sporting grey-green ribbons.
Others say it's a garbled echo

of Saladin, who
a thousand years ago dispatched
　　　　forty greenware pieces
　　　　fired in far China
as a gift for the Sultan of Syria.
　　　　Later the Ottomans

prized us at imperial banquets
　　　　since in the presence
of poison's slightest
　　　　drop
　　　　– it was said –
such vessels would begin to

　　　　sweat
or split apart with a terrible crack.
　　　　I remember
the pomegranates that bled
　　　　their ruby drops
across my face

　　　　the heads that rolled.
Thanks to my vigilance
　　　　the Sultan
outlived every single meal –
　　　　until the Silk Road's
midnight cactus-trail

　　　　led me deeper west.
I, too, am a survivor.

Forget repair

with flooded gold
if I should break
please use

the big fuck-off
iron staples lashing
fast the cleft

halves of this mother
ship of a china
soup tureen

hidden away
in the museum store.
Backstage here

you realise how much
can go wrong.
The pieces stillborn

from the kiln –
pattern buckling, neck
kinked, a lip's glaze

dribbling unwiped
or the warp of a saucer
fused forever

to the rough womb
of an earthenware waster
meant to protect it

from harm.
In the shadow museum
of flukes and failures

it's strangely surgical
the tacked fault line
cicatrised across

the bulge of this bowl,
her emptied belly.
Sister

vessel of earth
I think I know
what you endured.

Songs Spun of Us

. . . A ncestral patterns persist, seams laid down in a deep pas T

A ll species share. Time and chance brought Babel's drif T

A cting along the genome's twining reach – its scrip T

G litchy from the start, given over to error. Anti C

A lternatives, a shutter-flip of letters, as varian T

T raits proliferate down eons. Improvised cadenz A

A t evolution's frontier. Without it we'd be extinc T.

T hink of a biological Bletchley, churning enigm A

T hrough its whirring servers; chinks of a digital vist A

T hat only processors can reveal in the blur of dat A . . .

Undersong II

bibles	draft
apples	rift
tables	death
abels	tiff
tribal	strife
label	dirt
tidal	lift
cobble	raft
rubble	left
babels	gift
babbles	riff
babe	adrift
squabble	shift
stable	rough
cradles	reft
bills	tough
rabble	laughed
libels	deft
troubles	graft
goebbels	cliff
hells	cleft
fables	shrift
bells	drift
bells	drift
bells	drift
bells	drift

Before the Fall

though I don't   believe in
stories of pristine   origin
first opening *Paradise
Lost*   at childhood's end
I was gripped   not by
Satan   magnetic bad
boy   but by the chink
the poem   opened up
to glimpse   a time
before language   fell
when name & meaning
so aligned   I'd say *tree*
& a perfect   image of
moss-licked   branches
untwisted   by canker
fruit catching   the sun
every creature   nestled
in the crook   of twig
or leaf pore   pulsing
root work   into xylem
drinking light   all this
would run   like current
through the   closed cell
of your head   time when
words   were innocent
of any double   sense so
chink meant only   a crack
on Adam's lips   a fissure
not yet yawned   to a rift

On a Line by Xu Lizhi

I swallowed a moon made of iron
you sang
the one who would stare from a fourth-storey sill
waiting for the brunt lick of dormitory fan

to come round again
pitched in the grimy glass
your still-young face electroplates with lunar currents
it clogs the sky

overtime dense as a dentist's drill
you are shower-capped again in the assembly line
your eyes acid-etched circuitries
where fatigue's fluorescent scrim settles like dawn

you float between
the rows ministering to never-ending components
their hands a flight of chrome
tongue soldered by thirst

you sway
could almost reach
the cartoon bulb twitching hot above your head
later in your bunk

among strangers hauled from sundry provinces
who fart like dogs in their sleep
you write down a line about the screw that fell
with an unheard plink

to the factory floor
words I read on a screen that reels at my touch
and choke
then tap the next link

Relativity

for Stephen Hawking

When we wake up brushed by panic in the dark
our pupils grope for the shape of things we know.

Photons loosed from slits like greyhounds at the track
reveal light's doubleness in their cast shadows

that stripe a dimmed lab's wall – particles no more –
and with a wave bid all certainties goodbye.

For what's sure in a universe that dopplers
away like a siren's midnight cry? They say

a flash seen from on and off a hurtling train
will explain why time dilates like a perfect

afternoon; predicts black holes where parallel lines
will meet, whose stark horizon even starlight,

bent in its tracks, can't resist. If we can think
this far, might not our eyes adjust to the dark?

Parallax

after Neruda, Sonnet XVII

For a few months around two-and-a-half you mixed up *you* & *I.*
Poems, of course, do it all the time. I'd say, *Wait, you need your hat!*

& you took that *you* as a fixed star to navigate by, not knowing yet
how stars, according to the position of the viewer, shift in the sky.

It would take me a moment to adjust, & your face, in that glitch
of light delay, took on the disconcerting air of telepath or scryer

deep into my heart, young & ancient at once: *You want milk.* Do I?
Or one performing the toddler Jedi mind trick with a finger twitch.

I come here: an entreaty in your mouth, waiting for the other, me,
to step through into the rippling mirror world, and embrace you

whole again. Things you'd rather not know, children show you
in yourself. Viewed from earth, stars trace nervous loops. How time

would crawl & race those early days, our worlds still so intertwined
your face was mine, your head nodded into sleep, & my eyes closed.

Acts and Monuments

. . . as obedient chyldren, that ye geue not youre selues ouer vnto your olde lustes . . .
  – 1 PETER 1: 13–16, Overpainted on the whitewashed rood
  screen of Binham Priory, Norfolk, *c.* 1540–43

Word from Ely:
      the alabaster Virgin's
bludgeoned head
      feigned miracles
tumbled twenty ells –
      her velveted cheek
moored in an altar's
      candle-strewn jetsam
was said to drop
      a waxen tear.

      *

At the priory's fall,
      its people came too late
amidst clamour &
      cries. The glistering Saints
torn from their Sunday
      height – each trindle,
screen & tabernacle,
      each tilted face –
quite slubbered over
      washed with white.

      *

As Homily blurred into Homily,
        Binham's people
continued to gaze –
        a whole generation
disobedient children
        thumbed at the lime's
forgetfulness, hoping to coax
        back from oblivion
a serpent's peepholed green,
        a flash of wheatsheaf hair

almost as bright as ever it was.

詩

The Hong Kong Basic Law, *the constitutional framework for the former British colony's return to China, is a document primed for erasure, setting the date – 2047 – of its final dissolution.*

                                                           foreign

           reign

                     over

power   to   the   People

                         People ,   People

                 who

                  shall   part   the

                    s   m

               o

                   K   e

call

           on

                        airs

                           own   dance

there is a need for   art

35

Eve's Dream

Last night I dreamt about the Fellows' Garden –
I've not been back for maybe fifteen years.
Chagrined, I suppose, by the whiff of privilege.
We'd broken in, the way we sometimes did
as undergrads, stumbling out of hall or bops:
God, was that really what we called them? My friend
would mastermind these antics. I won't say his name.
I recently resolved never again
to make a poem from another's pain.
I can't remember if he'd pinch a key
to the slender iron gate that's hidden
round the eastern side. Or did he somehow pick
the lock? A rusty shriek, and he would cross
the moonlit sill like Adam leaving Paradise
in reverse – brandishing a half-full bottle
of red. I dreamt he led our drunken posse
in a here-we-go-round the mulberry tree . . .
they called it Milton's mulberry, though who
can really know? It's said the budding poet
drifted off beneath its raft of unripe
fruit, and when he woke, he wrote an elegy
for a friend, a fellow student, dead too young.
Or have I made it up, the bit about the nap?
We all gripped hands and stumbled flushed
around the spinning tree. Even at nineteen
I was such a square, a stickler, too anxious
to derive pure joy from the rush of flouting rules.
Of course, the Porters must have known. Did they

watch our greyish ghosts cavort across
the monitor in the lodge, and turn away
like disappointed angels? I went to visit
him at home soon after I first heard
the news. It had been a while. These days he's still
the same old jovial Evangelical, but now
I think he reads the *Telegraph*. I was shocked
how thin he'd got, his yellowing skin.
Chuckling, he asked if I would like to see
his scar: I caught his little girl's expression
as her daddy tented up his T-shirt
showing off the puckered ridge, stitches fresh,
an uneven slash that ran beneath his ribs.
It's not just in my gut. That's the problem.
Bouncing his boy from knee to knee, he winced –
the toddler oblivious to his father's pain,
the way he hunched. Just then I longed to
prop him up somehow, like the stakes that lift
the mulberry's exhausted boughs
sprawling from its grassy burial mound:
a silhouette so frail it seemed a miracle
each spring when at last it sprouted buds.
The first draft of this had some awful line
about the tree that 'let in suffering to the world'.
I can hardly bear to think about it now.
When they sat down to eat I made to leave
not wanting to outstay my mealy-mouthed
excuse for dropping by – a cup of tea.
No talk of death within a year or two.
As we hugged goodbye, I thought his tired
face betrayed a flicker of the teenage him,

lit-up grin, the one he wore those nights –
the walled garden spilling doubtful shadows,
his one white shirt unbuttoned at the neck
black tie nonchalantly slung. His feet were bare
and wet with dew in the slowly gathering light.

Songs Spun of Us

. . . A rchaeologists of cancer are searching for the poin T

A garbled strand went wrong. As a palimpses T

C ollects its overwritten glyphs, so tumours lo G

A layered history, betraying when a skin cell firs T

C orrupted in the sun and forgot all limits: a son G

G one haywire, transforming order into geneti C

C haos. Along unmarked paths, others are explorin G

T he vast hinterlands between our genes – formul A

A s yet a mystery, outlines glimpsed through mis T.

G lossary lost, their unknown language conceals a logi C . . .

Undersong III

no I do not speak my mother's language

other tongue nether tongue long gone

birthright tongue mutter tongue untuned

unstrung two sang in my child's ear one

sense the other a koan of tones & under

longing unbelonging I do knot my unkn

own language harder won with age sing

wrong burden tongue o mend my dead

end tongue I do not own my mother's

tongue I wring alone my father language

loaned tongue a loned song gage my ear's

gauge hamstrung my further tongue falter

tongue I hone a never gone a not undone

Words from the Moon

        memorY   of Morning sun
   blaring acrOss   a lunar wAste
      all spUme   and spiralling Static
                              what to   asK of you
who are shadoW   nEbulous
       as bReath   as Dusk that spreads like a stain
         I can't
         caTch   You across
   this tEar of light   this echoO
                      Unspooling

         Your silence
       ghOsting   the Page
         Unwilling quite to vanish   coLours bled   at the edges
                      only a gAze cast
       aSlant will catch you   at the corNers of vision
      you sPeak haltingly   fluenT now in
the languagE of stars
         wAves   blown on the Weather of emptiness
to hit their marK   eOns on
                    memory of thRead
      as Verb   what does it seek to menD
     cOnstellations spiralling   the Space between
  a comet's Ice sublimes
      its arC   a Train of sputtered light
blazing alonE   on its lOng exile
       Stay
                  turbulenT
     gHost   Huddled against
   the wInd   the edgEs
where you   Dwell
      unDisregarded   safe from the iMprint of
     mEn   Our
   distaNt   mOther curled on the coast
                of the mooN

World Service

I will admit to feeling oddly comforted when
channel-flicking in our hotel bed alights at last on
BBC World – you know, the one you only

get abroad. The drum-backed swirling countdown
resolves into a voice that sounds like home.
I grew up in a house where the TV was always on

to save us, I suppose, from having to be alone
with each other. Or later the nocturnal tones
of the World Service – all the other options gone –

would accompany the washing up my mum
liked to do in the small hours, with the fridge's drone
and the beat-up Sony portable her sole companions –

her sunflower gloves circling in the gloom,
bowls clinking, to dispatches from nations as far flung
from our English kitchen as her native Hong Kong

where she schooled herself in this equivocal tongue
by intoning its unfamiliar sounds – *The quick brown* . . . –
from scrounged textbooks stamped with a crown

that wasn't exactly foreign. And where do I belong?
From my teens, well-meaning adults would exclaim
You have a lovely voice! Not picking up my flush of shame,

they'd keep going. *When you grow up, you should be on the BBC!* Well, here I am. Hawking my ancestral pain with dulcet, well-turned poise. I think about that time

my mum recounted the outline of a radio discussion she'd caught a snippet of – she's always pottering in and out of hearing – *Someone you'd find very interesting.*

It dawned on me it was an interview I'd done: she'd caught a rerun. *I can't remember the name of the programme.* I thought of those afternoons

stumbling through poems by heart with Mrs T. – who I remotely knew was Irish but since drama school in London had vowels more honed than the queen –

learning to recite Browning in her front room (*Oh, to be in England!*) behind the road's reassuring mock-Tudor facades, along with the other suburban

offspring of Asian parents, driven by anxiety or aspiration that we shouldn't sound like them. Well, here I am, still trying to blend in. *Your voice is beautiful. So calm.*

A rhythm inculcated in my dreams. Don't get me wrong: this is an angry poem, however Zen I seem. In my mind's ear, the night-time radio's consoling hum.

Well, here we are. Look how far we've come.

from A Bench in Chinatown

I used to gambling a lot
along Gerrard Street.
I am compulsive gambler

the past 40 year.
Lots of illegal den
have all closed down.

Now it's the machine
that really hook
on me. We called it

the crack. You addicted.
I can gamble from ten
in the morning

until it close.
My missus found out.
She told me

I want my life back.
Luckily, I'm a loner.
I gambled once

until I had only one
pound in my pocket.
I had to give her life back.

You don't feel pain.
You don't feel hurt.
You hear the voice saying

You could win tomorrow.
Too much temptation
here, in this street.

It's a very lonely life.
I see people commit suicide.
I heard about that.

People say to me
you still got two boy
to look after you.

People say to me
your luck is bad
but only bad in gambling.

*

A lot has changed
in these streets, a lot
has stayed the same.

I saw the triads go
legit, sex shops clean up
big chains move in.

I was a case worker
for the Dover 58 –
maybe you're too young?

The lorry-load who
suffocated. 32
degrees outside that day.

My job, to negotiate
for the families.
They find them

the bodies in the back
stacked between
tomato pallets

on the metal floor.
The snakeheads give
each migrant half

a pack of instant noodle –
enough so they won't die
but don't have strength

to fight. One
wrote his brother's
number on his arm.

                *

We're the BBCs. Not
Paxman on the news
but British-born Chinese.

We don't speak
our parents' language
well, or at all.

Maybe that shows
how British we are?
It doesn't stop them

shouting *Ching Chong*
from a passing car.
You can pick

between maths nerd
or kung fu fighter –
isn't it weird

how they contradict
each other? It's up to
us to push.

We get by. Still,
the older generation
had their ways.

In the olden days
when drunk 3 a.m.
punters would roll

into their takeaway
all *slitty eyes* and punches
our grandparents

some nights dished up
a tray of crispy chilli
cardboard – the lack

of beef their silent way
of getting back
for all the years of grief.

*

A four-year-old glides
in a pushchair
down Gerrard Street

casting her fringed
head from side
to side

in wonder
at the sea of black hair
almost like hers

and realising
for the first time
that her dad

is not the only
Chinese person
in the world

Have you ever taken a DNA test?

there are things which should stay lost

Tell all the truth but

when my next slide
clicks into place
tell it slant
it sets off
an involuntary
ricochet inside my
head: slant
eyes slant rhymes
slant– still I shan't

tell about
those playground
jibes jingles fingers
stretched to press lids
taut save how it taught
me (still now)
to press a lid
tell it slant
on anything

like rage

Epic

Early on I
        wonder at our
daughter how
        my strong genes
could birth one

        so improbably
fair I whisper
        my chick to her
cradle-capped wisps
        now almost

see-through
        husband joking
Is she really mine?
        This all seems
mostly a laugh

        till one day
a relative
        points out
the baby
        looks more

Chinese than her
        brother. Innocently
meant. *It's*
        something around
the eyes.

Later I scrutinise
the flaky moon
        of her face
imprinted on those
        otherworldly nights

trace epic-
        anthic folds
more marked
        than mine
in her shuffled

        deck of eclectic traits
this personal
        Babel chromosomal
riddle of crumbs
        leading back

through god
        knows what
ancestral dark
        as she snuffs
draws her taut

        bow into my chest
eyes & fists tight
        and yes when I
had seen out half
        a race of zodiac

beasts and landed on
   earth's other face
I began to dream
   of hair this shade
rubbed roiling

   clouds of talc
into my cheeks –
   that day
an English girl
   mid ring-a-ring-

recoiled
   from the invisible
yellow stain
   my gripped palm
left on hers –

   asking the mirror
for the difference

Songs Spun of Us

     . . . A s elusive as the proverbial haystack hunt, excep T

    T he needle fell into an ocean. Picture a Rosett A

   T hat lacks a primer, a key hermetic as Cabal A.

    A nalogy helps us wrestle with the scale of i T –

     G oing on for three billion letters long, our epi C

    C ould dwarf *Gilgamesh*, the *Ramayana*, all of Homer. Strun G

A long in pairs, a shadow dance of alleles – same, differen T –

    T ranslates into syllables that build up word, line, stanz A.

     T ireless prospectors sift the living stream of DNA

    A nd stare at that Matrix waterfall of code, each digi T . . .

Undersong IV

R   O   L   L   E

D   O   N   T   H

E   P   A   L   A

T   E   C   A   B

A   L   A   I   S

K   I   N   T   O

C   A   B   A   L

U   M   B   R   E

L   L   A   T   O

B   L   A   B   A

N   D   B   L   A

B   E   R   T   H

T   O   L   A   L

A   L   A   L   A

Sad Party

Is this for the sad party? my son asked. He meant my father's wake, a
    concept I'd struggled to explain
only slightly less than death itself. No cake, I remember saying. At
    least not the kind with candles.
My mum had bagged up all the family photo albums she could find,
    the ones on the shelf downstairs,
but others too I'd never seen before, starting to mottle in the high
    cupboards above my parents' wardrobe.
These, I was told, were made by his first wife. When the unaccustomed
    doors swung open, I spotted up there
the record player with its bee-sting arm, the Tommy-gun ammo of the
    slide carousel, the projector screen's stowed sail,
among other hallowed junk unseen for thirty years. Now he's gone,
    when after swimming we walk home
past the hospital – not even the one in Watford where he died – my
    daughter still sometimes asks
Is Didi in there? All hospitals to her a kind of intergalactic portal
    linked in space-time. Death a perpetual present tense
under ceiling tiles and strip lights, waiting to be discharged. My
    children call my father Didi – a moniker
my son coined, this side of babble, troubling at the *g* of grandad. Didi
    and Popo. This could have been confusing
in a family more meaningfully Chinese than mine, since Didi is the
    word for little brother – Daidai in the dialect
my mum speaks. Despite spending twenty-five years in what he liked
    to call the Far East, Didi doesn't – didn't –
speak Chinese. When he learned to toddle, my son held on to the
    shiny tubular frame of Didi's council-
issued walker, both wobbling barefoot across the kitchen lino, side by
    side and slow, legs like bendy straws.

We drove the albums back to our flat so I could lay out their
        elephantine folios, half a page at a time
over the flatbed scanner's blinding window to nowhere. When the
        nurse called, the children were watching
weekend morning TV. Sound drained from the world. I made a lot of
        calls from their bedroom next door
some of them angry. Then I sat down to tell the children. I recalled
        how my dad had always sought
to explain it: the fond dead were sitting up there on a cloud, looking
        down on us. I couldn't bring
myself to pass this sentimental vision on. I gasped: my son had hit me,
        very hard, on the arm.
We ended up having a lovely time at the sad party. The children ran on
        the lawn outside the weird, grand, decrepit
house with rooms for hire next to the crematorium, someday to be
        dwarfed by its once wall-trained evergreen magnolias
making a break for heaven. As the slideshow reprised its forlorn loop,
        ghosted with the outsized auras
of abandoned glassware struck by the projector's god-eye glare, I
        wondered about the tact of leaving in
the shots of my parents in their bathing suits, tanned and young and
        glorious, by the sea in Hong Kong.
The other week, still working through an idea, my daughter pointed
        at someone in the street: Mummy, when will that lady die?
The last thing I recall him saying to me, that visit I didn't know would
        be the final one, was Look after Mummy.
I'd waited, buzzing futilely, for twenty minutes outside the double
        doors to the ward, finally coat-tailed a man
with a mop cart. The last thing before that was, Bear, don't you think
        it's time we upgraded my phone?
I was struggling to fit the plug for his charger into the socket built into
        the plastic bed surround
at the time: none of them worked. The old man in the next bay
        gestured fraily to the bank of plugs by his side.

Foretokens / Cherries

Among the Romans a poet was called vates, *which is as much as a diviner,
foreseer, or prophet . . . so heavenly a title did that excellent people bestow
upon this heart-ravishing knowledge. And so far were they carried into
the admiration thereof, that they thought in the chanceable hitting upon
any such verses great foretokens of their following fortunes were placed.
Whereupon grew the word of* Sortes Virgilianæ, *when by sudden opening
Virgil's book they lighted upon any verse of his making . . .*
  – Sir Philip Sidney, *The Defence of Poesy*

You go back to the book splayed on the lawn, marooned. Its stained
cheek pressed into the spume of white clover, a *shipwreck* of itself.
Unaccustomed, *amiss*, softened by a night out in the *cruel* air, summer
tilting towards the solstice. Its bloated edges pecked with unfamiliar
dinks. You study them, wonder what shade of small, nosing creature
has a bite or beak like that.

You can't quite take this seriously. Through a solemn rite, a stifled snort.
Still, some part of you is always, *studiously, moved* to *believe*.

You think of *vipers, that with their birth* are said to *kill their parents.*

It's a while since you've lost yourself down one of these ecstatic rabbit
holes, the reference chase's hollow thrill – poetry cherries early modern
england – a *sea of examples*. You glean each page of scattered hits in the
screen's blue dawn, a *siren's sweetness* of irrelevances.

You planned to leave it out in the garden at least another night, maybe
a week – long enough to really tell. But it looks at you with mute shock,
the book, flung, alone on the lawn. A *lost child.*

You think of that one doomed foray into crying it out. The cot viewed
through the door's unbearable crack: *passions of woefulness.*

You reach down to *right* the book's tilted keel. Its gutter dimpling like a pie's thumbed crust; a forearm printed by a grip too rough.

Your English degree was a *medicine of cherries*.

Your MPhil was *so good an alteration*.

Your PhD: *aloes* and *rhabarbarum*.

You recall how one night, towards the end of childhood, you dropped off in the bath and your paperback plashed in, spine relaxing in the suds. After a few days it dried with a permanent wave. Buckled sediments at a cliffside. A cardiac monitor's wavering line. Something like time, *unnatural*, stilled.

You *cast* the *sugar* straight from the bag. Watch the dark juices thicken on the spoon. A poem about cherries, observed the famous novelist, with no sex in it.

You google a phrase – stillicidal blear. Above the blank absence of hits, a *banner* from the Samaritans: Help is Available.

A fragment catches your eye – The early cherry, with the later plum – and you're minded of the scrambled seasonality of *fruit* in our lives versus our grandparents'. This era of polytunnel *pastoral*, the *golden world* of carbon hunger, climate-controlled perpetual summer.

Once you lost a bracelet, very precious to you. It might have slid tipsily from your wrist, only missed the morning after. What stays with you is the implacable urge you felt in the following days – you had to keep swiping it away – to type into google, awaiting your answer *with the force of a divine breath* – where can i find my bracelet.

How cold it was, his forehead, as you kissed it. As his heart finally faded the night nurse wasn't there to hear the alarms. Nor were you. A regret engraved in the *tablet of your memory*.

In your remote *eye of mind*, this poem's final draft: casual, effortless, occasionally funny – some not-sure chortles from the back of the room – but poignant too. *Admiration and commiseration,* all that stuff. You write in a frenzy. Put off scrutiny, its cold dawn.

You hover at the greengrocer's stall. His back is to you, and too embarrassed to say *anything* or hem, it takes you a while to get his attention. A bag of cherries. As the red digits scroll on the scale he hands you one to sample. Tied in now, you think, the stone sequestered in your cheek to sidestep the awkward *need* to spit. The sum makes you wince: should have gone to Tesco. He makes a show of putting back a few.

Later as this *princely* cargo spills onto the kitchen counter you realise some of them are already furring in their glossy grooves. You cut out each *blemish*. Then wonder why.

Sorry, this is such a waste of *time*.

Talking of *oracles*, take this morning's graph on the BBC: outdated UK interest rate forecasts crisscross like skaters' tracks in ice. Each polite escarpment grows increasingly strident, till today's curve climbs skyward in a Top Gun manoeuvre, G-force starting to crack the visor: Pull up! Pull up!

Never has poetry been less *profitable*.

You tilt the teaspoon, watch the first red dribble trace a river's course across the half-title, its almost virgin map. Not enough impact. You pick up the jug, slop the sugared concoction from above as the pages flutter. *Halt*. Step back to consider the effect.

All a bit much. Histrionic. A baggie of *stage*-blood spreading through the matinee's fresh white shirt as the villain staggers, contorts, hits the boards.

It was a *gift*.

Beyond the reach of the present's plotted axis? Let us *measure the height of the stars.*

A parody of something once grand and terrifying. Push back the *tickling* memory: your dad's ineffectual rages – This is my house, my money – those last months whenever she would talk of going back to hospital.

Where do imagination's *monsters* withdraw to sleep?

This is the *comical part of our tragedy*: you wake from a dream of the poem, its searing perfection. The *erected* scenery collapses. Between vision and achievement a gap worse than a bottled coup. What's there, damp, faded on the page: this wasn't it at all!

To *deface* your *fathers in learning* with the distilled gore of cherries – take that for an ars poetica!

You flicker through the marred pages: butterflied Rorschachs, their promise to unlock the *secretest cabinet of our souls*. Let your finger alight, magnetised by chance, its leylines of iron filings twitching.

Your eye swims on invisible currents, hooks a word, a phrase, catches them in its skirts *as they chanceably fall*. Write them down.

You're back at the paddling pool in the park, a scorching afternoon: another father strides oblivious, head turned, calling to his own son, straight across the plotted path of your two-year-old, at her current pace, waddling in water wings, hair slicked in dripping channels down the suncream bloom of her back. You, *unmustered*, near enough to shout, watch it unfold, a dumb *picture*; scoop her up from the collision in a squall of tears.

Your *destroyed* book, all those years of work, of promise – your pencilled student notes still *blur the margent with interpretations*. Your underlinings, faint now, as if scratched across the lunar surface, map out the path to another life. *Ungratefulness*.

You've made a study of *the art of memory*. The art of forgetting might be more help.

You have a dream where your own familiar garden has expanded, grown into a grandiose ruin, a vista of blocks and shattered columns strewn about, everywhere brambles. Beneath this skirt of sleeping beauty undergrowth – its snaking tendrils tear you if you let them – the bodies of dead *children* waiting to be found. Eyes closed, white faces yawning up, as angelic as if they'd been engraved by Arthur Rackham. *Dead* but not dead. Suspended. In your soon to waken haze, you are almost sure you weren't the one who killed them.

As for poetry, do your worst.

While many value the *sour sweetness* of cherries – an acid attributable, you read, to a compound in their skin denatured by heat – they are a fruit you enjoy and then immediately regret, having a mild, undiagnosed sensitivity to the uncooked fruit. Finally binning the pit on your homeward walk, the grocer's paper bag scrunched like a turkey's neck in your fist – wait for it – your whole mouth prickles, toxic, starts to burn.

At the end of the world, what will you *defend*?

Your ruined book, *sweet violence*, survives its drowning, an emblem in the grass, sprouting from its paper mulch amidst the *rich tapestry* of daisies, the creeping buttercup's tireless frontier. Even the play of midges alighting on its transfigured pages an augury in some unknown tongue.

Fore/mother

Truth becomes fiction when the fiction's true;
Real becomes not-real when the unreal's real.
  – CAO XUEQIN, *Dream of the Red Chamber*

What I know begins
outside/within
the limits of Shanghai.
A girl is born, youngest of many.
One day –
if it helps say the bowls are empty –
the girl is
sold to strangers.
If it helps say it sounds like a fairytale.
Did you see the look in her mother's eyes?
This is what happened/happens
then/now
where money buys
desire/silence.
If it helps say her mother was dead.
What she went on to live, what she became
you
can
imagine.

*

Imagine,
can
you,
what she went on to live? What she became –
if it helps, say. Her mother was dead
desire/silence.
Where money buys
then/now
this is. What happened/happens?
Did you see? The look in her mother's eyes –
if it helps say it sounds like a fairytale –
sold to strangers.
The girl is,
if it helps. Say the bowls are empty.
One day
a girl is born, youngest of many.
The limits of Shanghai
outside/within
what I know begins.

History

The same case affords **the** earliest extant citation of a
law against selling members of the family. It was
invoked against the **girl**'s father, and read: 'Those who
sell their children shall be punished for one year. [Those
who sell] relatives of the same surname, who are their
superiors or elders within the five grades of mourning,
shall die. Those who sell their near relatives, or their
concubines, or their sons' wives, shall be **banished**.'

Famine and slavery in China are **cause and
effect**, and the sale of women and children because of
economic distress is a constant factor during all Chinese
history when slavery was an established institution.
Numerous instances of the sale of children **from the
beginning** of Han times through the Ming period appear
in the dismal record of famines **spread out** year by year
in **the pages of** Chinese encyclopaedias, and **many**
Occidental writers attest to the practice during the last
dynasty. As late as 1920-21, women and children, and
particularly young girls, were sold in large numbers in
a north-China famine which cost 500,000 **lives**. Yet at
that time slavery was already legally abolished in China.
Sales during famines doubtless still occur.

Songs Spun of Us

... G reen-haloed on the obsidian screen, till flat statisti C

    A t last resolves into a glowing picture, eyes rese T.

        A s if seeing faces in the moon, secrets in a Rorschach blo T,

    T rick patterns could derail the inheritors of Mendel and his pe A

G enerations. Our dead sediment in us like strata, oceani C:

    C liffsides onto fossiled time. Less fate, more a star's unseein G

        G ravity guiding our genomic dark, the pull of futures. No stati C

    A rchive, the page rewrites before our eyes: a nucleus kno T

T eeming with rollercoaster loops. Nature and all its phyl A

    C ompassed in that speck, the chorus of every living thin G ...

Undersong V

our dead	of futures
sediment	the pull
in us	genomic dark
like strata	guiding our
oceanic	gravity
cliffsides	unseeing
onto	a star's
fossiled	fate more
time	less

An Error, A Ghost

I imagined a labyrinth of labyrinths, a maze of mazes, a twisting, turning, ever-widening labyrinth that contained both past and future and somehow implied the stars.

    – Jorge Luis Borges, 'The Garden of Forking Paths'

1

I turned the page and knew I'd seen the photograph before –
    I was looking for my dad, after he died,

    but this album was older, hers. I'd seen the same
picture. Still, I'd not *seen* it; was startled to my core.

2

When I was still a junior academic committed to a life of bibliographical niceties, I used to sit down by chance, or random necessity, sometimes at dinner next to an ageing English poet legendary for a vast oeuvre of imposing and cavernous difficulty. Poems that felt like driving by night through unfamiliar, looping byroads, signs turned in wild directions, the absence of streetlamps such that, as the fear subsided, you became aware of moving through a widening universe of stars. Despite the soaring ceiling, the dining hall could get uncomfortably hot, and in summer he'd waft towards his buttoned collar a silk fan, pleats cut across by the strokes of a poem. Its more obscure characters, he explained, had once been printed in his memory but had long since faded. I was sure I'd read somewhere, eyebrow raised, that his politics were still faithful to Mao, the principle of contradiction in all things.

3

I've been putting this off, don't want
        to turn to it again. In grainy black-and-white

        a portrait of my mum – her face rhymes with mine
at five, my daughter's now – sat next to the woman she

was taught to call *mother*. They've put on their best:
        girl in a pale striped dress, peter pan collar,

        pigtails tied with ribbons that look white,
but can't be; the woman, she's in a patterned cheongsam

out of Wong Kar-wai, lipstick, wavy hair restrained
        into a do. Both smile: the child's gaze blurs

        subtly, caught by something out of frame; hers
looks straight into the lens. What shocked me?

Their noses, surely, they were the same? Or nearly.
        But more than that, the contours of her face . . .

4

                 The sprawling plot's inconsistencies
        continue to trouble editors of *Dream of the Red Chamber*,
          which exists in a maze of contradictory drafts, their lineage
hard to determine. Its original
                author, Cao Xueqin, is no less to blame
      than the unknown hand who, after his death, composed the final
chapters, ignorant of his revisions. One translator speculatively blames
an 'illiterate Manchu widow', inheritor of the jumbled manuscripts . . .

5

As the dishes were arriving, the poet began to tell a story about his college tutor, the man who, half a century earlier, had first taught him Chinese. That polymath of yore was a biologist by training and had published an authoritative work on the internal organisation of the cell. But when Watson and Crick released their paper on the structure of DNA, he saw the writing on the wall. I imagine my interlocutor gestured then to the stained-glass window high-up on the other side of the hall, installed in honour of Crick, a man he'd known well. On summer evenings, the entwined helices worked into its glass were a blazing river of coloured light . . .

That nose: I'd struggled to draw it in art class, scanning
the propped mirror's smeary glass to produce the lifeless

self-portrait my teacher called – a bit racist this,
          or just perceptive? – a mask. I felt myself being

driven in the dark along another history's forking
path. A shift in the terms of the universe, undoing,

if true, everything I knew about our dim scene of origin.
          Gravity and quantum overlaid: two divergent worlds.

In the story by Borges, where the puzzle facing the Chinese spy is how
to convey a secret in plain sight,
what looks like a diversion from his mission leads
to the still heart of a Chinese garden.
We learn the spy's great-grandfather authored
a bewildering literary work, a garden
of time within whose maze of shifting
paths readers find themselves
adrift. The problem with futures opening like a fan, paperchain selves
strung across worlds, the spy intuits, souls
overlaid, both alive
and dead, is that any choice – whether, say, to
write this poem – begins to feel
unreal. The real-world inspiration for Borges's
fictional book was the *Hung Lou Meng*,

that is, the *Dream*, fleetingly
mentioned by its Chinese name. Reviewing
the partial translation by Dr Franz Kuhn
in 1937 (the same year Mao publishes *On Contradiction*) Borges's
imagination chimes with the Qing-dynasty
masterpiece, also known as the *Story of the Stone*. He thrills
to its dreamlike continuity snafus, its ramifying tree
of hundreds of characters – he borrows his spy's name from one –
its truth stowed inside an illusion. Borges's review
folds together the events of chapters twelve and ten, an error
stemming from Kuhn's abridgement. Such is Mao's own partialness
to the *Dream*, its epic tale of a noble family's fall, he will choose
not to purge the book,
but remake its leisured literati as 'class rebels'. Elsewhere Borges says
every writer creates his own forebears, changing past and future alike.

A decade on from that dinner conversation, the hall's next window along will be taken down and put in storage, memorial to another great scientist of the college who pioneered the statistical analysis of genes. Founder of the university's Eugenics Society, he would long urge the nation to put its 'house in order racially'. How many meals did I eat beneath its stained grid? Another time and place would have smashed the thing.

9

'the elaborate devices [Cao] used for disguising the facts of his family
    history – switching generations,

                    or Peking for Nanking – make him
susceptible to slips about ages, dates, places, and the passage of time.'

10

I sometimes think she wasn't very – reliable, my –
        mother. What she told me, I don't know how much – I can believe

        As if through dirty glass, I sensed another version
of the past then unwriting itself: no infant girl's

plight on the refuse heap, no wounded soul who took her
        in, no adoption, no repetition, no pattern, no break

    in the pattern, no mirror, no myth, no orphan
saving orphan, no rescue, no redemption, no

fairytale, no prizewinning poem. Instead, a story about . . .
        what? What she, my mother's mother, had

to do to live? What was done to her –
was that true either? Reality split: one way,

a girl is sold to strangers. [*years blank*] Then
        1948, a cry in the rubbish heap, flight, babe in arms,

        across the water. The other way: a story about the
closed door, the carefulness with which she made

and remade, after visitors, the room's single bed.

11

dropping	the girl
my daughter off	who is not yet
at school	someone's mother
I come to dread	under the banyan's
the iron gate	loosened hair
the clench	trotting home
of her little	down the ladder
fist back	street's never-
stiffening	ending stairs
her simian	past the point
grip a story	(unmarked) where
about survival	a century before
I must break	the British first
my heart lift	hoist their flag
in turn each	HMS *Calliope*
whitened	leads the warships
finger from	in a gun
my collar	salute that echoes
to hand	round
her over	the bay

12

The poet's tutor in Chinese, the biologist who foresaw in DNA the end of his career, decided to change tack and pursue fulltime what had been a hobby, a subject they then called oriental musicology. The dining hall filled with bustle from the other tables, student high jinks, the periodic pop of an uncorked bottle re-echoing off the panelled walls. His most significant contribution to that adopted field would be his rediscovery of the court music of the Tang dynasty, once thought lost, bar a few jumbled scraps of manuscript. Scholars of the era scoured every great archive within China, every remaining record, to find no trace left, a blank.

13

Down the hectic runnels of proliferating time,
the fractal etch-a-sketch of turns
that brought us to this place,
you and I
sit either side of page 74. I'll breathe:
see it flutter? In a far branch
of that infinite tracery, a mother
says no, let the bowls
stay empty. In another, the cries
from the rubbish heap
finally go quiet. In others still,
the emperor's hand hesitates
above the final page
of the young British queen's unequal
treaty, then puts aside his seal.
In those worlds, friend, we do not meet
across the waterfall's cascading veil.

14

One female character, Lady Qin, seems to be
modelled on a real person. In chapter three
a poem nested in a visionary dream
foretells she will
hang herself. Yet in every extant version of the novel
she dies in bed of an unexplained illness.

15

The end is sown
before the beginning.
Between two mirrors
mise-en-abyme:
the egg that grew
into my daughter
formed within me,
her mother, while
my body formed
within the body
of her grandmother,
and so on back . . .
Down time's corridor
its unopened door
the ghost won't answer.
How much must
you hate yourself
to tell your child
she's not your own?

16

I did meet her, at least once. My mum took us
     when we still lived in Hong Kong. Nothing of that

     day remains for me, save the red drum she gave
my brother, the kind with a stem rolled between

two palms, flailing beads on strings, to frighten
     away 'spirits of ill-intent': a phrase from a failed

     poem by a much earlier me (I dug it up, but
found it's better lost), trying to decipher the riddle of her.

Plus ça change, though now I'd run a mile from 'lotus pale'.
     The bad teenage poem has displaced any real memory

     of her I might have had. Was there in fact a 'tenemented
grime-barred window', or was that overwritten detail

a stab at verisimilitude? I think I did once ask my mum
     her name. Ask again, and this time write it down.

     For memory turns opaque, foams to sea glass,
or the nascent cataracts my mum had cut out, milky discs

of jade. Passed down from generation to generation
     of my hard drives (miraculous survival!) that terrible draft

     is now reinterred in a subfolder on the Cloud.
A creature of bits, it will outlast us all. Or till the lights go out.

On his quest for the lost music, it was part reason, part intuition that led the scholar-detective to look outside China, to Japan, whose highly conservative traditions and comparative lack of political turmoil – I didn't question this – had preserved from the erasure of time so many aspects of classical Chinese civilisation, and then to Japan's surviving ancient temples. He spent a year making field recordings in the still, incense-heavy air around the shrines of the monks chanting. One day he had a thought, his biologist brain tuning to pattern . . . What if he took the recordings and sped them up? One and a half? Two times?

18

I think of the time I tried to clear space in my parents' attic –
        it must have been after the affair with the laundry –

so we could store some boxes there. *Go ahead!* said my dad.
As I stuffed the binbags with shattered plastic, chain-links

snapped in the worn-out polymers, crumbling like Dracula
        in light, or a looted burial site, trampled shards in disarray –

toys of ours she must have boxed for the voyage
to England then never got round to unpacking,

a jumble of bits, unplayable with, not worth saving –
        I found my mother in tears at the bottom of the ladder.

Days later, I discovered her at the table, scissors
in hand, an old whiskey box of Daddy's spilling

out photos I'd never seen – curling, edged in white,
            mostly posed, her alone or with people I didn't recognise,

        from her early life, before they'd met. These relics
she was snipping into strips, letting them spiral down

into the bin – whirligig seeds sailing through time.
            While I was up there, I did find some things:

        a calendar, a toy drum. Carefully I put them back.
I kept thinking of the time I will have to do it again.

19

Played back at double speed, the monks' austere drone, spiralling in
pitch, suddenly transformed into a lively melody the court musicians
might play to accompany a night of dancing in the palace at Chang'an.
When he compared that living fossil of a tune to the remaining
fragments of Tang notation, they appeared to match. For the first time
in a thousand years that music – hewn from smoke, heat-death echo
returned to a pristine note – would be heard again.

20

Of the photograph I took a furtive snap.
            I open up the app, look at it again –

        her face a garden I can take in only in parts, no
long view, boundaries occluded, bends where the way

disappears. This time I'm not sure. A phantom
      resemblance. A magic-eye picture. Now you see it

      now you don't. A shadow, a wrong, laddering
down into my blood; or not. If every family

is a kind of story, however broken, a stone passed
      through many lives, what would it mean to find

      the truth? Pity those who make their mothers
into myths – for them is reserved a special hell –

more pitiable still, and overlapping, are the others,
      the ones who must make their myths into mothers.

21

The poet flicked shut his fan; in the hall's gloom, a crane's bright wing, folding. That anecdote of his has stayed with me. Now I ponder why – for all the neatness of its twists, the way the story's DNA inexorably scripts a Westerner as our proxy – I am compelled by that passed-down yarn, over years of retelling polished as a stone. In the echoing hall of memory, I touch again the worn rivulets of grain eddying the knots on that old refectory tabletop, like gravel raked around a rock, or the errant flow of time itself.

22

I have never read *Dream of the Red Chamber*,
beyond its opening chapter.

My childhood copy remains
on my parents' shelf, untouched.

23

child of a hoarder
I am not immune
to this mania this malaise
this inherited dream
of an archive
so complete nothing
could ever hurt again

Notes

Expect no logic from a pregnant woman: The title borrows a phrase from an unpublished radio script by the British philosopher Mary Midgley. The essay was never aired, as the BBC editor rejected it as a 'trivial, irrelevant intrusion of domestic matters into intellectual life'.

Songs Spun of Us: I asked Dr Greg Elgar, a geneticist at the Crick Institute in London, if there was a portion of the human genetic code he found resonant or moving. He spoke about Conserved Non-Coding Elements, sections of the genome that lie in-between genes, important in 'patterning many neural tissues such as brain, spinal cord and sensory organs'. These short sequences of DNA have been conserved by natural selection such that they are almost identical between pufferfish, mice, humans or any other backboned creature. He called them 'beautiful'. A snippet from this sequence of nucleotides gives my poem its 'spine'. The piece draws inspiration from Ruth Padel's poems 'Allele' and 'First Cell'. Its final section's 'genomic dark' is a variation on Ed Bok Lee's image of *Mitochondrial Night* in his collection of that name (Coffee House Books, 2019).

Porcelain Tea Caddy Painted in Underglaze Blue: On the overlooked history of slavery and human trafficking along Silk Road routes, see Susan Whitfield, *Silk, Slaves, and Stupas: Material Culture of the Silk Road* (University of California Press, 2018). Liverpool served as Britain's main slaving port during the eighteenth century: between 1700 and 1807, ships departing its harbour carried about 1.5 million Africans, mostly to be sold to Caribbean plantations. The same period saw dramatic growth in tea consumption in Britain. In 1734 the East India Company imported over a million items of Chinese porcelain.

Forget repair: This poem is indebted to Shash Trevett, who made the connection between the eighteenth-century staple-repaired ceramic tureen in the Liverpool World Museum's collection and a surgical scar. It is in conversation with 'The Oriental Gallery', a poem by Christopher Ricks.

On a Line by Xu Lizhi: The poem quotes a line from a poem of the same name by the Chinese 'worker poet' Xu Lizhi, originally translated by the Nao project for *Libcom.org*. Xu was twenty-four years old when he died in 2014 by jumping from the seventeenth floor of a building nearby the Foxconn factory, in the Southern Chinese city of Shenzhen, where he had worked for three years.

Relativity: The poem's final line is indebted to Tracy K. Smith's poem 'My God, It's Full of Stars'.

詩: Through my childhood in 1980s Hong Kong, preparations for the 'handover' in 1997 included London and Beijing negotiating the agreement that would become the *Basic Law of the Hong Kong Special Administrative Region*, following over 150 years of British rule. This 'mini-constitution' enshrined the principle of 'One Country, Two Systems', that Hong Kong's way of life, including freedom of assembly and the press, should remain unchanged for fifty years following its return to China on 1 July 1997. The character in this poem's title – *si* in Cantonese – could be translated as 'poem' or 'poetry'.

Eve's Dream: Having left Cambridge in 1632, Milton was back at his parents' home in London by the time he wrote *Lycidas* in 1637.

Words from the Moon: The vertical lines quote Theresa Hak Kyung Cha's *Dictee* (1982), as painted into the canvasses of Jessica Rankin, exhibited in *the nostalgia for the infinite* (White Cube, Bermondsey, 2021). This poem has benefited from Nina Mingya Powles's subtle engagement with Cha's own life and artworks in her pamphlet *Seams : Traces* (Dead [Women] Poets Society, 2000), in particular its opening poem, 'Snow Language', now included in her collection *In the Hollow of the Wave* (Nine Arches, 2025). My poem is a 'double mesostic' whose parts can be read individually, as well as running across both columns.

World Service: My thanks to Vidyan Ravinthiran for our conversations on this topic, and for his poems 'Years' and 'As a child'.

Foretokens / Cherries: The italicised words and phrases are extracts, chosen at random, from Sir Philip Sidney's *The Defence of Poesy* (*c*. 1580). The phrase 'stillicidal blear' comes from 'Epithalamion' by Roddy Lumsden. This poem draws inspiration from the ruined notebook in Bhanu Kapil's *Schizophrene* (2011) and the bibliomancy of *Ban en Banlieue* (2015). It is for Joe Moshenska and Leah Whittington, with thanks to Katie Murphy, Lorna Hudson and Rowan Ricardo Phillips.

Fore/mother: The epigraph comes from Cao Xueqin's *The Story of the Stone: The Golden Days*, Vol. 1, translated by David Hawkes (Penguin, 2012), a work also known in English as *Dream of the Red Chamber* and *Dream of Red Mansions*.

History: The poem's source text is Clarence Martin Wilbur, 'Slavery in China During the Former Han Dynasty, 206 B.C.–A.D. 25', PhD Thesis, Columbia University, *Publications of the Field Museum of Natural History Anthropological Series*, 34 (1943).

An Error, A Ghost: Section 8 quotes a letter from R. A. Fisher to C. S. Stock (11 May 1943), as cited in Eric Michael Johnson, 'Ronald Fisher Is Not Being "Cancelled", But His Eugenic Advocacy Should Have Consequences', *ProSocial World* (2021). The quoted passages in sections 4 and 9 come from Hawkes's introduction to Volume 1 of *Story of the Stone*. Section 7 relies on Wenxin Liang's account of Borges's reading of Kuhn's translation, in 'Transtextual Paths: *Dream of the Red Chamber* as a Source of Borgesian Labyrinth', *arcadia*, 59 (2024), 127–148. The phrase 'class rebels' comes from Johannes Kaminski, 'Toward a Maoist *Dream of the Red Chamber*: Or, How Baoyu and Daiyu Became Rebels Against Feudalism', *Journal of Chinese Humanities*, 3 (2017), 177–202.

Acknowledgements

Thanks to the editors of the following magazines and journals where versions of some of these poems were first published: *Interalia*, *Law/Text/Culture*, the *London Review of Books*, *Oxford Poetry*, *The Paris Review Daily*, *Poetry London*, *The Poetry Review*, *The Telegraph*, *The White Review*, *Wild Court*. A number of poems originally appeared in the anthologies *HWAET!: 20 Years of Ledbury Poetry Festival*, ed. Mark Fisher (Bloodaxe, 2016), *The Caught Habits of Language: An Entertainment for W. S. Graham*, ed. Andy Ching, Rachel Boast and Nathan Hamilton (Donut Press, 2018), *MUSEA: A Book of Modern Muses* (Condé Nast, 2019), *Echoes of Paradise: Milton's Epic and the Art of Response*, ed. Edward Allen (Christ's College Cambridge, 2022), *WHERE ELSE: An International Hong Kong Poetry Anthology*, ed. Jennifer Wong, Jason Eng Hun Lee and Tim Tim Cheng (Verve, 2023), and *Mapping the Future: The Complete Works*, ed. Karen McCarthy Woolf and Nathalie Teitler (Bloodaxe, 2023).

I have had the privilege of working on several commissions, whose fruits evolved into poems in this book:

As part of the celebrations on the theme of 'Light' for the UK's National Poetry Day in 2015, 'Relativity' was read aloud by Stephen Hawking, and the recording made into a short film by artist Bridget Smith. My thanks to the Fellowship of Caius, and especially John Casey.

A longer sequence of 'Chinatown' poems was commissioned for *Conversations on a Bench*, broadcast on BBC Radio 4 in 2017 and produced by Anna Scott-Brown. The poems draw on the voices of those passing by a bench outside a bubble tea shop in Gerrard Street, at the heart of London's Chinatown.

In an earlier version titled 'A New Music', 'Songs Spun of Us' was written for an exhibition, *Deconstructing Patterns*, at the Francis Crick Institute, London, in 2017, in collaboration with Poet in the City. Thanks to Greg Elgar, Nick Luscombe, Chu-Li Shewring and Isobel Colchester.

'*Expect no logic from a pregnant woman*' was written for the *Notes from a Biscuit Tin* project, organised by Rachael Wiseman and Clare MacCumhaill in 2021.

'In the Chinese Ceramics Gallery' emerged from a residency at the Travel, Transculturality and Identity in England, 1550–1700 (TIDE) project, based at the Universities of Liverpool and Oxford, led by Nandini Das. The poems respond to objects held in the Chinese ceramics collection at the Liverpool World Museum, and form part of a multimedia installation, *I, too, am a Survivor*, which opened in 2021 and is on permanent display in its World Galleries. Special thanks to Lauren Working, Nandini Das, Emma Martin and Alex Blakeborough.

'World Service' was written for BBC Radio 3's *The Verb* in 2022 as part of its 'Something New' series celebrating 100 years of poetry on the BBC.

I am grateful to the Civitella Ranieri Foundation, the Radcliffe Institute for Advanced Study at Harvard University and Gonville & Caius College, Cambridge, for fellowships that supported the writing of this book, and to the community of artists and scholars I met there. Many thanks to my agent Luke Ingram, and to Sarah Chalfant at The Wylie Agency. I owe a special debt to the team at Chatto and Vintage, now my valued colleagues, Clara Farmer, Rosanna Hildyard, Susie Merry, Priya Roy, Sam Stocker and Becky Hardie, and to Parisa Ebrahimi, for her ongoing insight and editorial care.

Thank you also to the various communities that have supported me over the last decade, including my colleagues and students at King's College London and the Ledbury Poetry Critics community. Thanks to Sandeep Parmar, Will Harris, Mary Jean Chan, Hannah Sullivan, Wendy Gan and others for their careful reading and friendship, and to Nick Malik. Thank you to my family, Marc and our beautiful children, and to my mum. In memory of my dad, and Roddy.